W9-ASZ-677

Celestine

Drama Queen

Celestine
Drama Queen

PENNY IVES

ARTHUR A. LEVINE BOOKS
AN IMPRINT OF SCHOLASTIC INC.

Even before Celestine had hatched from her egg, the Duck family knew there was someone very special inside.

"Tappity-tap, tappity-tap," went the egg each day until –

crack!

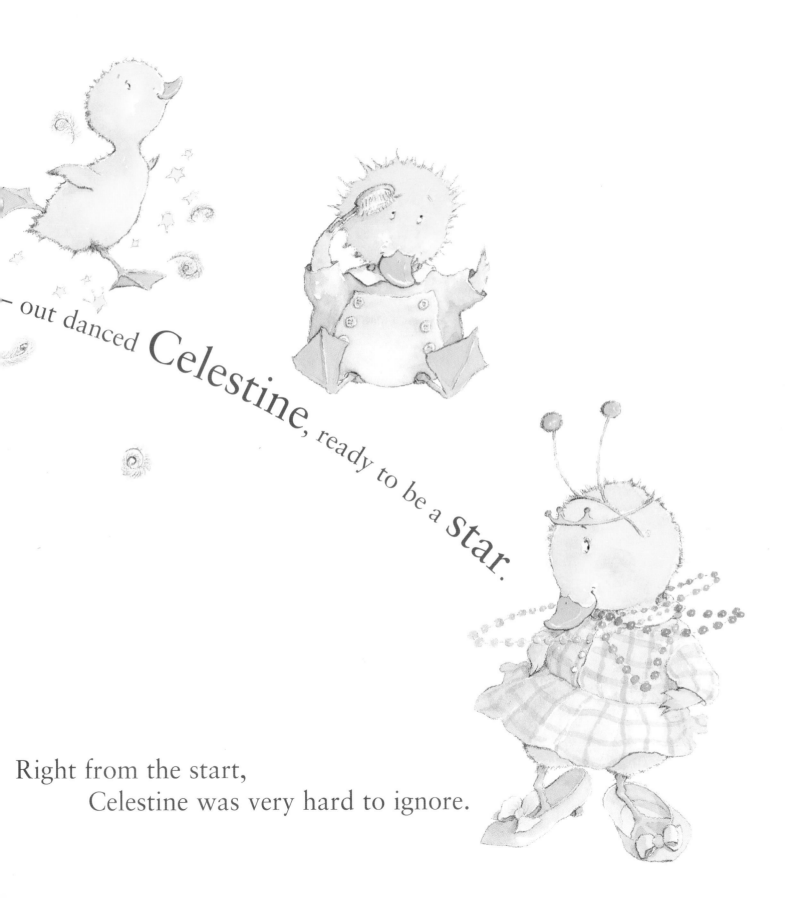

— out danced Celestine, ready to be a star.

Right from the start,
      Celestine was very hard to ignore.

As soon as she was old enough,
Celestine would dress herself
with great care, just as a real
star should.

Sometimes it
took a long time
to create **just** the right look.

One morning, Celestine swept in
to breakfast wearing her latest creation.

"Oh, Mommy! You know stars only eat
pink food!" she sighed as she looked
at her cereal.

"Do you think you should be wearing a tiara to school, Celestine?" her mother asked.

"Of course! A star must set an example," said Celestine, skipping out the door.

At school, Miss MacDonald took attendance.

"Archie?"

"Yes, Miss MacDonald."

"Beattie?"

"Yes, Miss MacDonald."

"Celestine?"

"Celestine's not here,"
answered Celestine.
"Today you may call me
Princess Druscilla Drake –
it's a much better name for a star, don't you think?"

"Well, Princess Druscilla Drake," said her teacher, "this morning we all have the chance to be someone else – we are going to begin rehearsals for our school play."

"I would be **delighted** to accept the lead role," beamed Celestine, twirling around the room.

"Thank you, Celestine," said Miss MacDonald. "There's an important part for **everyone**."

On the way home that afternoon, Celestine sighed, "Stars don't walk, they should ride. Especially when they've got the best part in a new play."

"And what **is** your part?" asked her brother.

"That's a **secret**," smiled Celestine,
                tap-dancing along the pavement.

After tea, Celestine rushed straight up to her room.
"I have to rehearse for the play now, Mommy," she
shouted, slamming her bedroom door shut.

"Want to rehearse your lines, Celestine?" called her mother through the door a little later.

"No, thank you," Celestine called back cheerfully. "They're very nearly perfect."

"Shall I help you practice?" asked her brother the following day.
"No, thank you," said Celestine,
"I know
every
word!"

The day of the play came at last.
Celestine breezed jauntily into
her classroom blowing kisses
into the air.

"How kind," she thought, noticing
some flowers nearby. "Someone has
sent me a bouquet!"

"But where is my red carpet?"
she wondered, walking down
to the auditorium.

"And the rest of the orchestra's late!"
she frowned, seeing only Mrs. Gobble
at her keyboard.

The moment had arrived.
All the little chicks and ducks huddled backstage.
The lights dimmed.
The audience grew quiet,
and the show began!

Celestine watched, trembling, behind the side
curtains, whispering along with every word.
"Time for you to go on now, dear,"
smiled Miss MacDonald.

But suddenly, Celestine's feet wouldn't work.
She was terrified!
"I feel **sick**," she coughed weakly.

"I'm going
to faint,"
she gasped.

"I won't!
I shan't!
I . . . I can't!"
she squeaked.

Miss MacDonald gently pushed her forward.
Celestine inched to the center of the stage,
her heart beating madly –

pitter-pat, pitter-pat.

She blinked at the bright lights;
she opened her beak . . .

. . . but nothing came out!

Celestine stood
quite still –
she couldn't
move a feather.

THE END!"

whispered
Miss MacDonald
from behind the curtain.
"Celestine, say your line!
Say 'THE END'!"

Then Mrs. Gobble flew to her rescue, striking up one last, fast, jazzy tune on the piano.

Quite of their own accord, Celestine's feet began to tap,

her knees bent,

and soon she was whirling and turning, skipping and spinning until, with one final leap . . .

. . . she fell to the floor,

a dizzy yellow triumph!

"Fantastic!"

"Encore!"

"Hurrah!"

The audience **loved** it!

"Well done!" they cheered,
clapping and clapping.

They all agreed it was a splendid
end to a wonderful show.

"Hurrah!"

"Brilliant!"

"Superb!"

But walking home, Celestine
was unusually quiet and thoughtful.

Flip-flop, flip-flop,
flapped her little feet.

"I'm still a star, aren't I, Mommy?
Even though I forgot my line?" she asked at bedtime,
a big tear dripping down her beak.

"Of course you are, my darling!" said Mrs. Duck,
buttoning up Celestine's pajamas.
"Just think of that marvelous dance you did!
And besides . . ."

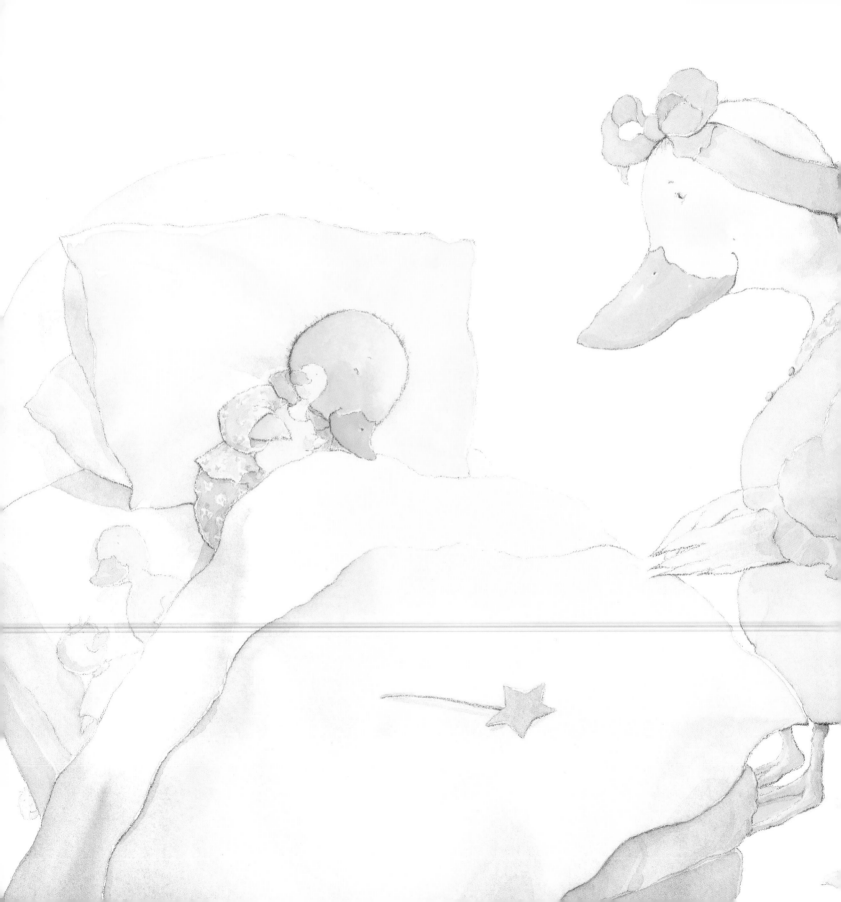

"... you'll **always** be a star to me!"
And she gave Celestine a kiss.

"Good night, little star,
good night."

Text and illustrations copyright © 2008 by Penny Ives

All rights reserved. Published by Arthur A. Levine Books, an imprint of Scholastic Inc., *Publishers since 1920*, by arrangement with Templar Publishing, an imprint of The Templar Company plc, The Granary, North Street, Surrey, RH4 1DN, England. SCHOLASTIC and the LANTERN LOGO are trademarks and/or registered trademarks of Scholastic Inc.

No part of this publication may be reproduced, stored in a retrieval system, or transmitted in any form or by any means, electronic, mechanical, photocopying, recording, or otherwise, without written permission of the publisher. For information regarding permission, write to Scholastic Inc., Attention: Permissions Department, 557 Broadway, New York, NY 10012.

Library of Congress Cataloging-in-Publication Data

Ives, Penny.
Celestine, drama queen / Penny Ives. — 1st American ed.
p. cm.
Summary: Celestine the duck is sure that she is destined for stardom,
but when her big break comes, she is temporarily stricken with stage fright.
ISBN 978-0-545-08149-8 (hardcover) [1. Stage fright—Fiction. 2. Ducks—Fiction.] I. Title.
PZ7.I949Ce 2009
[E] —dc22
2008008176

ISBN-13: 978-0-545-08149-8
ISBN-10: 0-545-08149-1

10 9 8 7 6 5 4 3 2 1   09 10 11 12 13

First American edition, March 2009
Printed in China